WISP

A Story of Hope

To Em and Tun,
For always, always understanding. – Z.F.

I would like to thank my wife, Linda, and children,
Albie, Flossie and Lillie, for all their love and support.

I want to dedicate this book to all those, wherever
they are, who hope and strive for better times. – G.B.S.

ORCHARD BOOKS
First published in Great Britain in 2018 by The Watts Publishing Group
10 9 8 7 6 5 4 3 2 1

Text © Zana Fraillon 2018
Illustrations © Grahame Baker-Smith 2018

The moral rights of the author and illustrator have been asserted.

A CIP catalogue record for this book is available from the British Library.

ISBN HB 978 1 40835 010 2 PB 978 1 40835 011 9

Printed and bound in China

FSC
www.fsc.org
MIX
Paper from
responsible sources
FSC® C104740

Orchard Books
An imprint of Hachette Children's Group
Part of The Watts Publishing Group Limited
Carmelite House, 50 Victoria Embankment, London EC4Y 0DZ

An Hachette UK Company
www.hachette.co.uk
www.hachettechildrens.co.uk

ORCHARD

WISP
A Story of
Hope

Zana Fraillon and
Grahame Baker-Smith

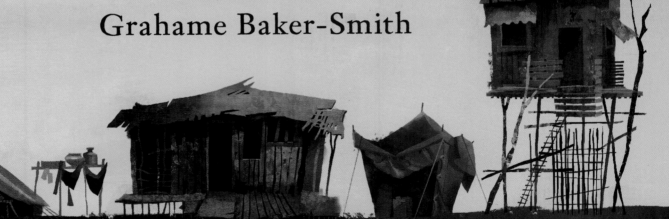

Idris lived in a small, small world.

A world where fences grew from the dirt and where shadows ruled.

A world with no trees to give shade,
no rivers to drink or seas to swim.

A world full of people, but
where everyone was alone.

Dust rose up in swarms around it, feet trampled it into the dirt, nobody noticed it.

Nobody, except Idris.

Until one day, a Wisp flew in on the evening wind.

Idris gentlied the Wisp from the ground. He softlied
away the dust and dirt and footprints.

And that was when he felt it.
The smallest whisper of want.

The Wisp began to wriggle. Flitting and fluttering,

it bustled Idris past rows of tents,

over the moonlit dirt

and along the fences' glare . . .

until it stilled at the feet
of a man, ancient and cracked.

"Is this yours?" Idris asked.

The man's eyes
were long ago
dulled, but he
took the Wisp
in his hands.

He held it to his ear.
Slowly, the spark of a
smile lit his lips.

"Once," he whispered.

The Wisp pulsed bright. The man lifted his voice, and music poured into the night. A swelling sea of rememberings twirled on the air and shimmered in the breeze.

The people stopped. They smiled, and together they listened to the blazing bright heartbeat of a song.

And when the man's voice quietened, there was just the hint of a hum in his step, and a bright in his eyes where the dullness no longer settled.

When the next Wisp
flew in on the evening
wind, Idris knew what
to do. He let himself
be bustled past and
over and along, until
the Wisp found who
it was seeking.

The woman looked at Idris, a sad etched
deep into her face. She held the Wisp to
her ear. A light flickered softly in her eyes.

"Once," she whispered, and the
Wisp quivered with delight.

The memories spun
from the woman's
fingers and rippled
through the air.

A forest blossomed
from the dirt and
pulled free a storm.

The people stopped.
They smiled, and
together they
watched as a thunder
of colours rained
down from the sky.

And when the woman's fingers stilled, there was just a splash of happy in her words, and the sad on her face was not as deep as before.

Then one evening, a Wisp appeared that
did not wriggle or flutter or flit.

Instead it settled at Idris's feet and Idris
wondered, was this Wisp meant for him?

He waited. And waited.

But no memories appeared.

Idris had lived his whole life in this small, small world. There was nothing else to remember.

Then Idris held the Wisp close.
Slowly his ache was calmed, and
a seed of understanding began
to grow deep inside his heart.

For Idris's Wisp wasn't
a memory . . .

It was a promise.

Idris felt his feet begin
to move and his arms
begin to shake. He
danced free his promise,
sending it shooting
from the stars and
bright soaking the dirt.

The people stopped.
They smiled and
together they felt the
promise of a dream.

Idris lifted his hands, and let his Wisp catch
on the wind. He watched it wing higher and
higher, flying over the fences to where people
had forgotten how to welcome wide feel.

It splashed in the rivers and danced in the
trees. It carried with it the heartbeat of
a song and the colours of rain, the scent
of new knowings, and the tremble of
stories from a thousand kingdoms.

The promise grew stronger with
each person it touched.

Soon, it whispered . . .